THE
LACE SNAIL

Written and illustrated by
BETSY BYARS

The Viking Press   New York

For Catherine

First Edition

Copyright © 1975 by Betsy Byars
All rights reserved
First published in 1975 by The Viking Press, Inc.
625 Madison Avenue, New York, N.Y. 10022
Published simultaneously in Canada by
The Macmillan Company of Canada Limited
Printed in U.S.A.

1   2   3   4   5   79   78   77   76   75

Library of Congress Cataloging in Publication Data.   Byars, Betsy
Cromer. The lace snail.   Summary: The animals beg the snail for
some of her lacy trail and she tries to oblige each with a gift appro-
priate to its nature. I. Title.   PZ7.B9836Lac   [E]   74-32376
ISBN 0-670-41614-2

The Lace Snail

Once a snail was on her way to the pond when she suddenly began to leave a trail of silken white lace behind.

The bugs were the first to notice. They said, "Look what the snail's doing!"

And, "Hey, the snail's making lace!"

And, "How do you do that, Snail?"

The snail stopped. She looked. She said quietly, "I don't know how I move. I don't know how I breathe. And I don't know how I make lace." She continued on her way. "It's just the way life is, I think."

The bugs ran after her, crying, "Listen, make us something, hear?"

The snail stopped again. She looked them over, one by one. She nodded. "You deserve lace as much as anybody."

And she made lace circles for the bugs, circles as light as the wind.

The bugs cried, "Hey, these things float!"

And, "Look at me, you guys."

And, "Whooo-eeee, I'm a bird!"

Below, the snail went quietly on her way, leaving a trail of silken white lace behind.

She had not gone far when she came upon a frog. A moment before, this had been the happiest frog in the world. "Hey, Bugs," he had just called. "Look at me! I got stilts!"

And the bugs had yelled back, "That's nothing, Frog, we got lace, man, LACE!"

After that the frog had not felt happy. He had been standing there, wondering where he could get some lace, when he saw the snail. He blinked and said, "Do you make lace just for yourself or can anybody get some?"

The snail stopped. She looked at the frog. She said, "You deserve lace as much as anybody."

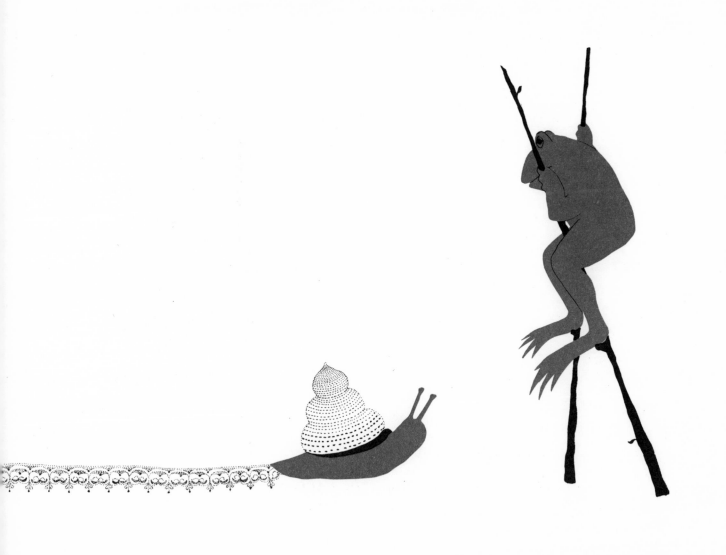

And she spun him a cape of lace,
long and fine and flowing. Then she went on her way.

"Hey, Bugs," the frog cried. "Now I got stilts AND lace. Look at me, you guys. I got EVERYTHING!"

The snail was passing beneath a tree when a snake appeared.

"You're losing something," the snake said. "There's a whole lot of something like lace spilling out behind you."

The snail said quietly, "I make lace."

"How? How do you do that?"

"I don't know," the snail replied. "I don't know how I move. I don't know how I breathe. And I don't know how I make lace." She continued on her way. "It's just the way life is, I think."

The snake coiled and said, "Make me something."

The snail hesitated. She looked at the snake. She nodded. "You deserve lace as much as anybody."

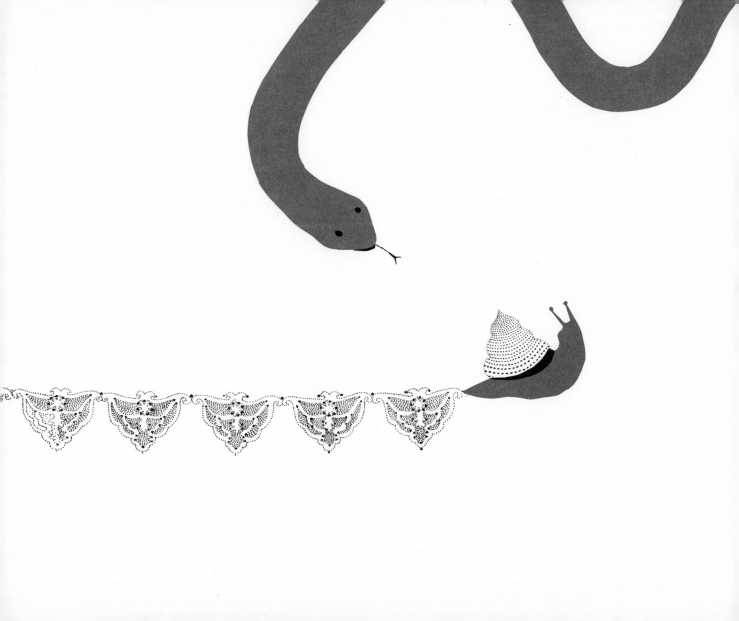

And she made lace bands for the snake, bands heavy with flowers and light with fine silken threads. Then she went on her way.

"But how does she do this wonderful thing?" the snake cried in amazement. "Look at me, everybody! I'm transformed!"

A turtle was waiting just around the bend. "I do not ask to be covered with lace," she said.

The snail nodded and continued on her way.

"However—"

The snail stopped.

"However"—the turtle continued—"as a mother, I cannot help but ask for a bit of lace for my beautiful children. And I'm not saying they're beautiful just because they're mine. They really ARE beautiful. And a little lace for each of them—well, it would be the answer to a mother's prayer."

The snail nodded. "The children deserve lace as much as anybody."

And the snail made lace hats for the children and one for the mother too. And then she went on her way, leaving a trail of silken white lace behind.

"Look at these beautiful children!" the turtle cried. "And I'm not saying they're beautiful just because they're mine! They really ARE beautiful!"

The snail had not gotten far when she heard a heavy rustling in the grass. She stopped. She looked up. There was a crocodile, waiting with open jaws.

There was a long moment while the snail looked at the crocodile and the crocodile looked at the snail.

Then the crocodile grinned and said, "Did I scare you? Boo! Did you think I was going to eat you?"

The snail nodded.

"Well, I probably WOULD eat you except that at the moment I am more interested in this lace, if you get what I mean."

The snail said, "You deserve lace as much as anybody."

And she made a hammock for the crocodile, a hammock of lace as delicate and as beautiful as a spider's web.

"I love it. I love it! I LOVE *it!" the crocodile cried. "And you can give me a push every time you go by, all right? Everybody can give me a push." He grinned. "Everybody* BETTER *give me a push, if you get what I mean."*

The snail nodded and continued on her way to the pond. She could see the water in the distance.

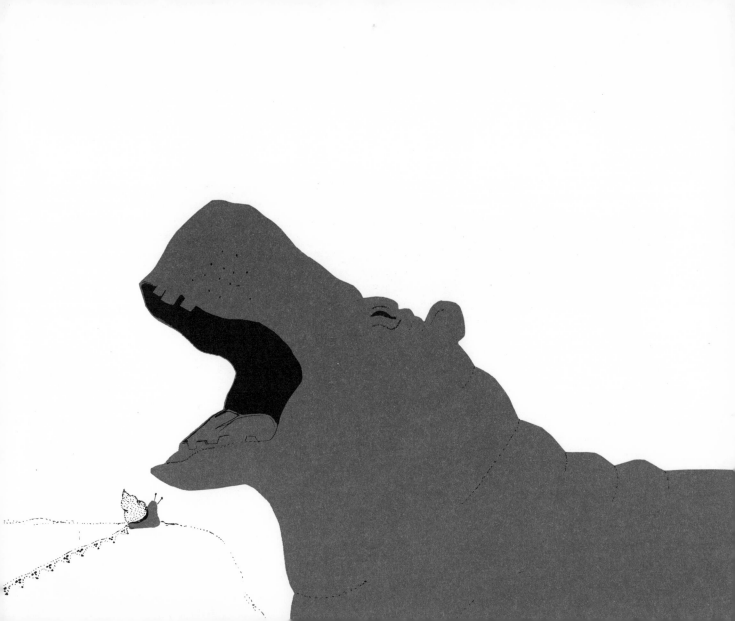

She was almost there when she suddenly heard one huge word and felt the heat of one huge breath.

"LACE!"

The snail looked up. It was a hippopotamus. "I want LACE!"

The snail pulled back into her shell a little.

"Am I too big for LACE?"

The snail looked at the hippopotamus. "You ARE big," she said.

"But TOO big? Am I too big? Or not too big?"

"You deserve lace as much as anybody."

And the snail made lace for the hippopotamus, heavy strong lace for the hippopotamus's size and light fine lace for the hippopotamus's nature.

Then she went on her way. She was very tired.

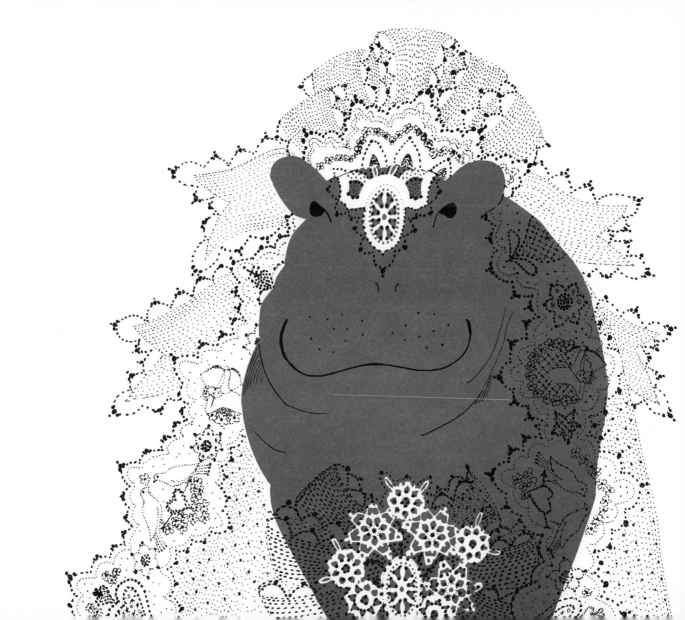

Suddenly the frog swooped over. He said, "Hey, Snail, how about making some capes for the bugs and making me a couple of these —" He broke off, and then he said in a louder voice, "Hey, stop. Wait a minute. You aren't making lace any more, did you know that? What happened, Snail?"

The snail turned. She looked. She said quietly, "I don't know why I move. I don't know why I breathe. And I don't know why I stopped making lace."

She continued on her way.

She could feel the cool moistness of the earth now. She glanced back once at the plain silken trail behind her.

She said, "It's just the way life is, I think." And she went to the water and rested.